But Bobby Grabbit
just laughs.

One day, Bobby Grabbit was taking Gracie to the zoo. He brought his swag bag with him, just in case.

"If you go robbing people," said Gracie, "I'll tell the zoo keeper to set the tiger on you."

But Bobby Grabbit just laughed again.

And when Gracie
wasn't looking,
he stole some fish
from the penguins . . .

and a rattle
from a baby . . .

and an egg from a snake . . .

and a hat from a lady . . .

and a key from the
zoo keeper's pocket.

When Gracie spotted what he was doing, she said:
"You are a very naughty daddy!"

But Bobby Grabbit was too busy stealing buns from the elephants.

So Gracie went to tell the zoo keeper.

"Mr Zoo Keeper!"
said Gracie Grabbit.
"My daddy is a very naughty
robber, and I need you to
set the tiger on him
right now!"

The zoo keeper was too high up to hear her. But someone else heard.

It was the tiger!

He opened one big eye, and saw what Bobby Grabbit was doing.

Then he opened the other big eye,
and saw what Gracie
was doing, too.

ICE CREAM

He saw her sneak everything
out of her dad's swag bag, so she could
give it back to everyone he'd robbed.

Except she got things a little bit mixed up.
She gave the fish to the baby.
"Waaa!" cried the baby, which
meant, "That's not my rattle!"

She gave the rattle to the snake.
"Hiss!" went the snake, which meant,
"That's not my egg!"

She gave the egg to the lady.
"Ooh!" said the lady.
"That's not my hat!"

She gave the hat to the penguins.
"*Honk!*" went the penguins,
which meant, "That's not our fish!"

And she gave a bun to the zoo keeper.
"*Thank you!*" said the zoo keeper,
who was very fond of buns.

She didn't know who the little key belonged to . . .

. . . so she hung it on a hook,
where the owner would find it.

Well, the owner didn't find it . . .
but the tiger did! He looked at that
little key, hanging just outside his door,
and he smiled a big tiger grin.

Then he reached out
a huge tiger paw . . .

. . . and turned
the little key
in the lock.

AND, MY!

Wasn't Bobby Grabbit surprised!

The tiger picked Bobby Grabbit up by the trousers
and gave him a good old shake to tell him off.
Everybody stared and went, "Tut, tut, tut!" very loudly.

Bobby Grabbit was very embarrassed.
"Sorry, everyone," he said. "Shall I give everything back?"
And everyone said, "Please do!"

So the tiger took Bobby Grabbit
around, and he gave back:

the fish to the penguins,

and the hat to the lady,

and the key
    to the zoo keeper.

The baby let the snake keep
the rattle, to make up for its
egg getting broken. And Bobby
gave the baby a bun instead.

There were plenty of buns left for the elephants, too.
Then Bobby Grabbit said: "I've been a naughty
old robber all my life, but it's fun giving things back."

"In that case," said the zoo keeper,
"I've got just the job for you," and he
handed Bobby Grabbit a bucket of fish.
"You can start right now."

From that day on, Bobby Grabbit worked at the zoo (and sometimes Gracie helped out.) They gave bananas to monkeys,

and fish to penguins,

and a bath to the bear,

and leaves to giraffes,

and plenty of buns to the elephants.

And what did they give the tiger?

A big old hug,
because now they were
the best of friends.

To Holly, Poppy, Frieda,
Harry and Evie

First published in the UK in 2015 by Alison Green Books
An imprint of Scholastic Children's Books
Euston House, 24 Eversholt Street, London NW1 1DB, UK
A division of Scholastic Ltd
www.scholastic.co.uk
London – New York – Toronto – Sydney – Auckland
Mexico City – New Delhi – Hong Kong

Copyright © 2015 Helen Stephens

HB ISBN: 978 1 407157 66 5
PB ISBN: 978 1 407158 04 4